Relax, Jax

Jeryl Christmas

This Book Belongs To

_____

This book is dedicated to my amazing
daughter, Lindsay Christmas Rowe,
and her precious son, Jackson,
my very relaxed Jax.

Relax, Jax. It's okay.

It's going to be an awesome day.

The sky is blue; the grass is green,

a better day you've never seen.

"But if it rains, I'll get all wet.
I think that is a likely threat--
dripping raincoat, soaking shoes,
soggy homework that I'll lose."

Relax, Jax. It's okay.

It's going to be an awesome day.

The sky is clear; the sun is bright,

a perfect day to fly a kite.

"But if my kite goes up too high,
I'll never see it in the sky.
It might get lassoed by a jet.
The pilot will be so upset."

Relax, Jax. It's okay.

It's going to be an awesome day.

The fish are jumping in the lake.

Cast a line and take a break.

"But if my line gets in a knot
or lands inside a flowerpot,
the fish will simply swim away
thankful for their getaway."

Relax, Jax. It's okay.

It's going to be an awesome day.

Go climb a tree up to the top

and watch the leaves and acorns drop.

"But if I climb and then get stuck,
they'll have to call a big firetruck
with sirens wailing down the street
while I'm left dangling by my feet."

Relax, Jax. It's okay.

It's going to be an awesome day.

Check out the circus or the fair.

Ride the rides without a care.

"But if I ride the ferris wheel,
it might go rolling down the hill.
Who will stop it? I don't know.
I might end up in Tokyo."

Relax, Jax. It's okay.

It's going to be an awesome day.

Go on a hike throughout the woods.

Take a backpack full of goods.

"But if I hike and start to stray,
I know I'll surely lose my way.
I'll likely find a big bear's den
welcomed by his toothy grin."

"YIKES!"

Relax, Jax. It's okay.

It's going to be an awesome day.

Think about your favorite dream

where people only eat ice cream.

"But if I dream and it comes true,
I'll be so sick like it's the flu.
I'll turn all different shades of green.
It will not be a pretty scene."

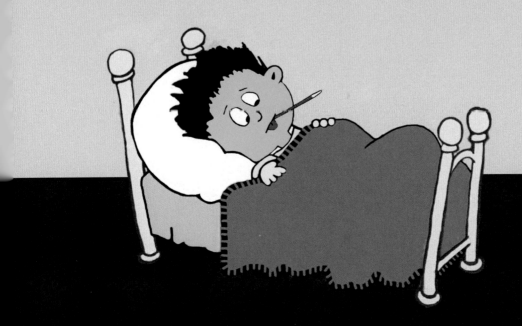

Relax, Jax. It's okay.
It's going to be an awesome day.
Go fly beneath a big balloon.
Why don't you go this afternoon!

"But if I fly in such a thing,
from the ropes I'll have to cling.
It might drift off in outer space.
I better pack a large suitcase."

Relax, Jax. It's okay.
It's going to be an awesome day.
Surf a wave, water ski,
scuba dive, or do all three.

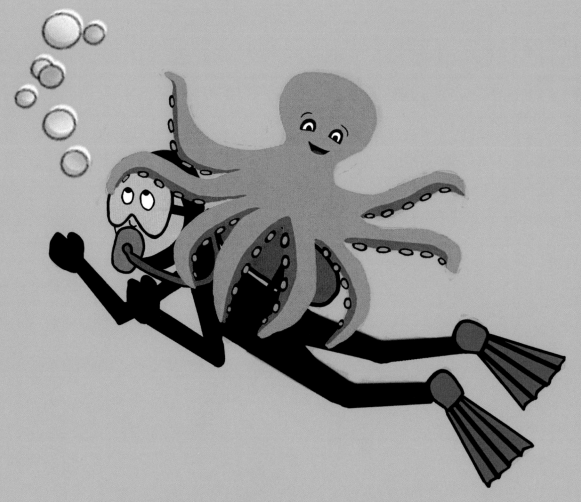

"But if I do those things at sea,
will anybody rescue me?
It really could be dangerous
if captured by an octopus."

Relax, Jax. It's okay.

It's going to be an awesome day.

Please don't worry anymore

of what **may** happen--what's in store.

"You're right! I **will** now try to be
filled with positivity.
The sky is blue; the grass is green,
a better day I've never seen!"

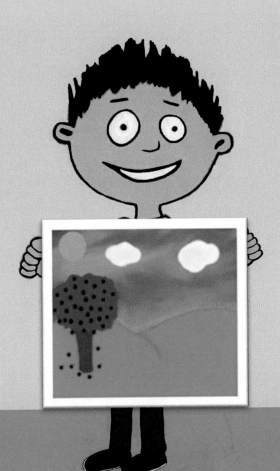

So...

Keep calm, Tom.

Just chill, Bill.

Don't fret, Rett.

Be still, Jill.

It's all good.

Learn from Jax.

Never stress...

Just Relax!

Made in the USA
Middletown, DE
21 May 2023

30783645R00018